OOPS
POUNCE
QUICK
RUN!

AN ALPHABET CAPER

To my mom

Balzer + Bray is an imprint of HarperCollins Publishers.

Oops, Pounce, Quick, Run! An Alphabet Caper
Copyright © 2016 by Mike Twohy
All rights reserved. Manufactured in China.

ISBN 978-0-06-237700-5

The artist used India ink and felt-tip pens to create the illustrations for this book.
Typography by Dana Fritts
15 16 17 18 19   SCP   10 9 8 7 6 5 4 3 2 1
❖
First Edition

Mike Twohy

OOPS POUNCE QUICK RUN!

AN ALPHABET CAPER

Balzer + Bray
An Imprint of HarperCollins*Publishers*

Asleep

Ball

Catch

Dog

Eye

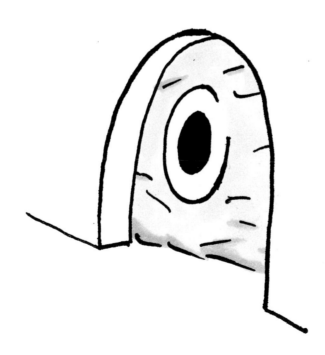

Feet

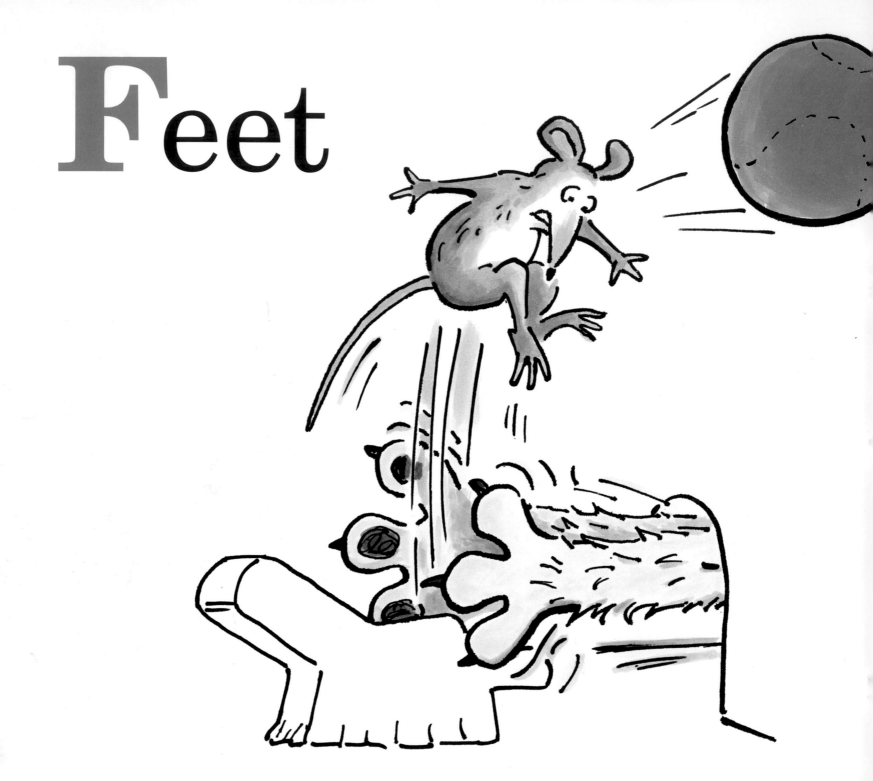

Help!

I'll chase!

Jump

Kitchen

Living room

Missing

Nowhere

Oops

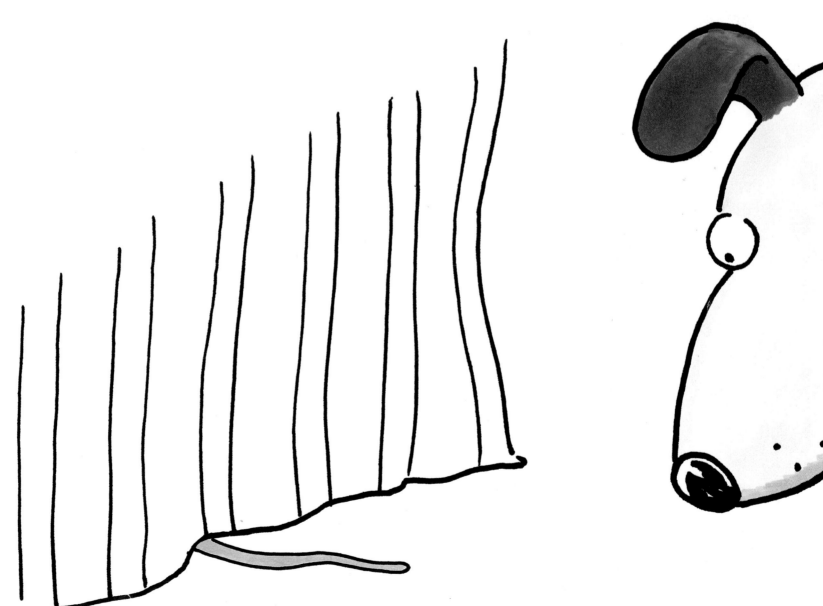

Pounce

Quick!

Run

Safe

To Dog

Unwrap

Very cool

Wag

Xoxo

Yes!